TEN TINY TALES
OF TERRIBLE WAR

David Tienter

book design and layout: SpiNDec, Port Saint Lucie, FL
cover image: David Tienter

Printed in the United States of America.

Published by Poetic Justice Books
Port Saint Lucie, Florida
www.poeticjusticebooks.com

ISBN: 978-1-950433-049

FIRST EDITION
10 9 8 7 6 5 4 3 2 1

TEN TINY TALES
OF TERRIBLE WAR

by
David Tienter

table of contents

TEN TINY TALES
OF TERRIBLE WAR

vietnam volunteer

12/31 2 P
"You did what?
Bastard. What about me?"
I try to explain.
Door slams
I get ready for duty.
1/1 2 P
She comes home
1/2   10 A
Forgetting not forgotten
Slushy winter day in Boston
I hate Boston
I hate the leaving
Trying to forget what's leaving
Empty and beaten I walk in slush
Wondering, can I bear the pain
Wondering why I feel so wonderful.

going in country

I've risen early to watch the sun rise over the East Indian Ocean. In the dark of early morning only a faint ship light reflects against the curling tops of waves. When the sun breaks the horizon, it turns the ocean a deep agate green and the waves' froth is crimson. This morning, an older Navy chief joins me in my vigil. He's enjoying a smoke before returning to work. The sea here is endlessly fascinating to watch. We both enjoy it.

He scans the sky for a minute, then turns to me. "It's going to rain today."

I believe he has read the sky and ask, "How can you tell?"

"It's monsoon season. Rains every day." He chuckles and returns to work. Smart Ass.

At nine o'clock I go below to help the ship's crew with sick call. It eases the burden on them and keeps my laboratory skills sharp. I'm aboard the USS Okinawa, a helicopter carrier that is being used as the staging area for my battalion.

Three decks down, I barely hear the announcement squawk from the ancient system.

"Tienter to aft-deck three. HM3 Tienter to aft-deck three."

I run to my space, pick up my pack, medical bags and rifle and begin to climb the stairs. I feel like I'm a spectator who has accidentally wandered on to a stage. I'm Rosencrantz or Guildenstern preparing to leave Denmark. I can see that I'm doomed but my actions have already been foretold by some crazy playwright bastard.

A large horned hand has slipped up from the mystical depths of hell to reach deep into my jungle fatigues and begins to squeeze my scrotum. "Run," the hand's owner commands me. "Nothing good can happen here, grim ugly disfigurement and death lie ahead for you."

I continue to walk steadily to my doom in shoes that have somehow become as heavy as cement. Each step takes all my strength. I know I should flee, but there is no place to go. I should hide, no place on a ship. Maybe if I just stay below, they would forget about me. If I fall and break my leg on these stairs, they would keep me here safe until it heals. Still steadily I climb to the aft-deck.

A Gunnery Sergeant holds up a hand, halting me inside the doorway. "Hold up, Doc. I'm getting your gear." He cannot see the terror that has gripped me, or he would have laughed, or talked, or helped me some way.

I show him my medical bag.

"You need your combat gear. Wait there."

He is dressed in what had been a freshly laundered and pressed uniform, but the heat and the action on the aft-deck had turned his uniform limp with large dark sweat spots enhancing the camo style fatigues he was wearing. Even his blocked cap was darkened around the brim. Still he carried himself in a way that clearly bespeaks his Marine Corps pride and inner strength.

He runs past me carrying gear, hoses the blood off it, and gives it to me.

"Get this on and get on that helicopter," he is pointing at a helicopter with its rotors turning. As I run to it, I pass a Marine on a stretcher. Doctors are working on him. He has lost his left leg below the knee. I realize where my gear has come from. All my fears have come true for the brave Marine on the stretcher.

My gear reeks from its covering of blood and cordite.

Thirty minutes later I am on the ground with my Company. I am embarking on the great adventure of my life.

purple heart

Late night monsoon rain
Black painted on everything
Crack, snap, boom, doom,
Corpsman up
Try to run. Fall too often
Crawl to injured man
Sucking chest wound
Tape shut with cellophane
Chopper lands, run for the lights
Lights go out
Pain digs me out of a deep hole
Alone in the dark,
Left leg locked to my chest
I push patella up from the side to top of knee.
Leg straightens, black reclaims me
I return alone, alone in the black
I hear "Doc"
Quietly I say "here"
Lieutenant Szabo has found me.
I won't die alone in a bomb crater
A.M. and light, I see my wounds,
I will live, I dress wounds
No medivac for me

senior corpsman

"How much?" I ask.
"Too much," sez Bob with his eyes.
"I can."
"You can't."
Five empty syrettes speak volumes
Bob can't speak
His jaw is gone
Ten months of bravery and sacrifice.
I stay out, his place
I will not enter
Damn tears, I walk on.

courage under fire

I watched, I learned
My Sergeant was tireless, fearless.
He led point, checked men's gear,
 dug up mines, helped everyone with everything.
In the worst of time, he was the best.
Quick with smile or joke
Ambushed one day, he stood tall
Encouraged the men to fight back,
"Get up, use those weapons
You're just as big a target
On your bellies as your feet."
A hero for all, a hero born
Op Meade River
Flew into hot zone, bullets cutting through grass.
Men running, men falling
Sarge ran back on the helicopter
Terror and fear are caustic weapons
Courage is not static.

1967

Day starts early. Black everywhere, I rise from the cot, throw on my flak jacket, grab my equipment, weapons, and move at double time to the Huey, joining with my team. Szabo is already there. Intel has been radioed in. A VC heavy has been located. We are being sent to snatch him, should return by noon. We carry no food, one canteen. The throb of the rotor is soothing and I quickly nod off. As always I sit on my helmet. Too many bullet holes in the Huey to think aluminum walls protect you. I carry an A-40 Sniper rifle, a .45 cal. pistol in a hip holster and a .38 cal. pistol in an ankle holster. I sling my medical bag over my right shoulder.

I'm a Navy Corpsman attached to the Marines. I love the Navy, but the Corps is my home. I have been lucky to be accepted into this elite group, Force Recon. More than two years of advanced training has been needed for me to be going on this mission. I may be going into hell, but it's with my brothers who can handle hell. I am not worried. Whatever happens, I can think of no greater honor than to be here with these men

Forward movement stops, ropes go out the door, Lt. Szabo checks the first man's rappelling gear. Less than a minute later, we are grouped on the ground, moving toward our objective. No talking now, only hand signals. Our eyes have adjusted to the dark, but we still need to be close to watch his hands.

By the time dawn begins to break, we are in position. I am twenty feet up a pine tree on the edge of the village where I can easily watch over everyone with the rifle.

They begin the search on the edge of the village. Sgt. Meese brings out six natives. They are passive and immediately go into the Vietnamese squat.

Then the first shot rings out. I see cone-hatted heads popping up everywhere. The Marines form a circle fighting outward. I drop the first five enemy that I can get into my sights, scramble down the tree and turn toward the Marines. I feel more than hear an explosion to my left. I am thrown to the ground on my right side. I've lost fingers off my left hand and it feels like the arm is fractured. White lights of pain guide me into the deep black of unconsciousness.

I wake up tied by my wrists to a bamboo pole. My arm is swollen but it's not bent. I'm glad it wasn't broken. In addition to my arm, I'm bleeding from at least five small holes on the left side of my body. Easy to see them, I am wearing no clothes. They have also taken my shoes. The powerful smell of gunpowder is harsh. The residue from the blast has coated the left side of my body. There are four other Americans tied to the pole with me. I don't know any of them. No idea what has happened to my team. Clearly I am a prisoner, I assume the worst, pray for survival.

We are the Show. VC propaganda on a stick. They lead us into a village and call everyone out. The elders just look at us. The kids poke at us with sticks and kick our legs. The younger people throw dirty water and call us GI's. Don't want to know what's in the water, but it smells like urine. I expect my wounds will be infected. We are marched through three villages the first day.

At twilight, we are given a half-cup of rice and, still tied to the pole, we are forced to sit on the river bank. The pole is secured between two large boulders. By stretching against the pole, we can just get our mouths to the water's edge so we can get some water mixed heavily with mud. Their leader, 'Uncle Ho,' comes by to tuck us in with a gentle boot to the head. Before nightfall the other prisoners are asleep. I sit up and begin to chew at the wire binding my wrists.

I'm in an awkward position, but if I do not escape, I know I'll be doomed. The insects will insure our death if the exposure, infections, or starvation does not kill us first. I chew on and try to break the wire. It's intensely painful to my teeth. I bend my wrists and arms, moving the wire with my teeth and gradually begin to feel it weaken. I lose one of my incisors, but I continue. I can always gum my food. First stay alive. Finally, I feel the wire break. I work one end of the wire around the pole with my mouth. I hurry knowing that if they come now, they will kill me. My mouth is bleeding freely now. The blood helps lube the wire and I slip one hand out and unwrap the other.

I hold one hand over the mouth of the man next to me and awaken him. "Silence is life," I tell him. I untie him. Much faster with hands. He is quiet and repeats what I have done for him to the next man. When both men are free and untying the man next to them, I slip into the river and quietly let the current take me downstream. I dog paddle to the deep channel and feel the current begin to pull me along quicker. Suddenly a sneeze, wild splashing then gunfire on the shore. Can't see what has happened. Can't help anybody. My heart wishes them the best. Hope some make it. A large branch floats past me and I pull myself up onto it. When light begins to break, I swim to the shore and enter the jungle. Traveling on the river is much easier, but I don't know where it's going or who is along the banks to to see me. I'm lost, naked, unarmed, and hungry. Not a good prospect for survival in enemy country. At least, I am well hydrated.

I crawl into the jungle a few yards and stop. I need to think. If I hurry now, I will die. If I panic, I die. I have only one weapon, my brain. I have to use it to survive. I stand and begin walking. Soon I find large leaves to wrap my feet. I tie them on with vines. Snakes are the easiest food to find and kill. Hoping they don't find and kill me first. I learn, I watch everything. It is safe to move when the animals and birds are quiet. If I move slowly, they don't react. If they are nervous, someone or something is moving. This is the land of water buffaloes and tigers. Buffs hate us and want to trample us. Tigers want to eat us. On the fourth day, I kill an enemy soldier. I know within seconds of seeing him that he is alone. I can smell the fear on him. Short timid steps, not long confident strides. He holds his rifle at the ready, too wary, too hesitant. A man leading a column of troops walks with his rifle at his side. He knows he's safe.

Once he passes where I am hidden, I step out, grip his head from behind and break his neck. Now I have a rifle with twelve rounds, a knife, and pants to wear. The pants are much too small but they are held up with vines and protect tender areas. I find the picture of a smiling Vietnamese cutie in his wallet. I think he was lucky to have such a beautiful wife. As I kill more soldiers later, I notice most have the same smiling picture. The picture probably comes with the wallet, or perhaps she is promised as a wife if he survives the war. His rations, such as they are help for a couple of days. His shoes are sandals made for children, and his jacket has a VC insignia. Death if I am caught wearing it. The biggie is the knife. Life is easier with a sharp blade. I use the sun for directions, move slowly and spend a lot of time worrying about tigers and find raw cobra to be the tastiest meat.

Three months later, I step out on highway 1 near Da Nang, in front of an armored patrol. They are not sure what to make of me, but the Marine Corps still remembers me. Hot food, medical exam, new clothes, and they call my folks to let them know I am still here among the living. It's great to be home again.

the cobra

The beast was throwing wake up-rays on me. Soon the heat would be unbearable, but now I could still function. This was the best time of the day. I stood rapidly, shook out my blanket, and secured it in my pack. Sleeping on the ground invited a myriad of nasty little beasts to snuggle in with any warm body. Many of them could kill a man with a single bite. Most Marines rose slowly, checking around them, whereas I rolled away and stood up, hoping I would get away before I could get bitten. It worked for me.

Grabbing my medical bag and rifle, I walked through the men to see if anyone needed anything. Today there was nothing too severe, so I worked on building a cup of coffee and lit my first, sat back leaning against my gear and traded friendly insults with the men.

The word soon came down: search and destroy.

The Vietnamese had buried large vats of rice in and around their villages to protect them from being taken by the Viet Cong. We would search the area, but through the years the villagers had become masters at hiding their goods.

I used a seven foot bamboo pole with a foot-long rice-sickle stuck into one end of it to probe the ground. The vats make a distinct sound when they were tapped. Actually, this was grunt work and I could have slacked off and hung near the company headquarters, but as much as I could, I worked with the men, had become close to them and no longer saw them as simple ground pounders. They knew what they were doing and were significantly effective in their actions. My satisfaction came from being respected by them.

True, I was only a corpsman and some disliked me because I had the power. The incredible power to approve them for medivac. By the third week out in the boons, almost all of the men had at least rashes, cuts, bites, and scrapes. In the states, most of them would be receiving medical care. Here they had only Corpsmen to count on. As senior Corpsman, I was the 'no' man. "You can make it today, let's see how you look tomorrow." They grumbled. Their right as enlisted men. Did I worry, yes, infections could spread rapidly, I never had sufficient antifungal cream and everyone had a rash. The food was crap, canned rations that were twenty years old, that combined with fear, constant heat, rain every thirty minutes, plus tramping through the rice patties, not enough water, and let's not forget Charlie, anyone of my Marines could be incapacitated by evening. Still, we had to have enough men to carry out our missions.

This day, I hit a vat within twenty minutes and it sounded like a large one. Chip, a marine from my platoon was next to me as I scraped the dirt off the lid of the vat. I cracked the top of the lid in with the butt end of my bamboo pole and bent over to see what it held.

A cobra, I swear it was at least 12 feet long, came shooting out of the vat. The venom from a snake that large would have killed me in seconds. I stood petrified as it crossed my boot and slithered away.

"You damn near bit the bullet that time, Dog," said Chip. He turned and smiled at me, then started humming the stupid little tune he was always humming and walked away, probing the ground again.

I followed him slowly. Legs shaking so hard it was

difficult to walk. I watched Chip continue to probe the ground while I watched. I didn't want to find another vat.

As he walked along, Chip stopped humming and began talking. He spoke softly so no one else could hear what he was saying. "Maybe you don't understand a few things about this place here yet."

"What're you talking about, Chip?"

"Talking about that snake, and Charlie, and all the rest of the crap here that's trying to kill us. Could be you and me are supposed to die over here."

"You're crazy as a mongoose in heat."

"Think about all the crap you did in your life. This was the kinda place you did anything to avoid. Now you here. It's just Karma coming back like a large penis to fuck you. Ain't nothing you can do when it comes. So quit being afraid of shit. Just do your job and don't worry, you catch it, you were meant to catch it. That's the beauty of Vietnam. I signed off on my ass when I flew in here. Now fear don't get me. The actions we take here will define our lives forever. We do what we can and protect our guys. You gotta remember, Dog, we are different. We are hated by more people than just about anyone on earth. Vietnamese hate us, most Americans hate us, Chinese hate us and Russia hates us. Hell, we are accepted by us and us only.

"We are the best. If we die being the best, that's probably a blessing for us." He looked at me, winked, and began to hum that miserable tune again as he walked off probing.

I almost believed him, except that I knew I was going to live through this. My legs still didn't work right as I followed Chip and began to probe again.

I heard a muffled explosion in the distance. It

sounded small, like maybe a grenade. I waited listening hard.

"Corpsman, Corpsman up."

I hurried back for my medical bag, then ran in the direction of the explosion. Peaches was shouting at me, "Over here, Dog, over here. It's Tarter that got hit. Hit something back with his e-tool."

"Thanks Peach," I said as I sailed past him.

Three Marines were helping Tarter walk back to our area. As I came up, they sat him on the ground.

"It's my eyes, Dog," he said. "Knew I shouldn't dig there, but Green wasn't listening to me. That little fucker, I knew I shouldn't have dug there, but you think he would listen to me?"

"Easy, my friend, easy. Let me get a look."

"I'm blind, dammit, how you think I can live blind."

"Well, let me see," I said, pulling his arms off his face.

"Hurts bad, hurts bad."

I emptied a morphine syrette in his leg. Opened his eyes to see how much damage was done. The blast had caught his face full on. The skin on his forehead and cheek were pockmarked. I opened his eyes and flushed them with canteen water and wrapped a bandage all around his head.

"I think you'll be okay. You going to need work from the doctors though, don't know as I did everything myself." While we waited for a medivac helicopter, I bandaged up a wound on his right hand and kept talking to try and alievate some of his anxiety.

Three marines walked him up to the LZ and boarded him. We Corpsmen never really know what happens to the men we treat, unless, of course, they die. I never heard from Tarter.

      Gathering my gear, I turned my mind from Tarter. I'd done my best and could do no more. Chip's advice had seemed strange, but Tarter's injury had caused me to lose my fear and I went from barely walking to full out running in seconds. Maybe Chip had a handle on life, after all.

smoke and mirrors

Firmament is the base we seek
Avoiding the void we seek solid ground
Sustaining both our being and our beliefs
We seek forever
"If I can have just this."
The ethereal dream of safety-surety-pain free
Still the largest ship sails rolling waves
Firmament. All solid and real or smoke
Put down hard with roaring hammers
A place for life
A tabernacle with gleaming towers high
A collage set in a copse of trees
If only life didn't move with water seeping
Pushing aging decaying
Dress them in bellbottoms
Coats of navy blue
Singapore beacons to us
We can face the Cape
Good hope for these fair winds
Make them climb the riggings
Fasten now the jib
Death we see is everywhere
Feel it now the ship is rocking
It's the sailors who pay the highest price
No firmament for lost sailors
They get a round of rum

We face the enemy
Thinking a meadow would smell sweet
Fire that cannon
A good port waits with a raucous bar maid
Short skirts and blackened teeth
The sailors final award
One who deals in fluids
Waiting now always waiting

dichotomy

A white-haired man moans softly,
A weak voice from a mold of blankets
Piled over a sidewalk grate,
Stops me on a city street.
"Where are you, Audie?
Alvin and you were torchbearers, both gone
Now when we need you. We're adrift.
Heros and murderers, together crew the ship
Excepting awards, all the same
Terrified men in bad times.
I got me a star me a star, huh,
But I never was a hunter of men.
They loved you on the line, 'Thank you for your service,'
Put flowers on your graves
Deep sorrow when you pass
They still hate us
 hate what we do
Ugly callous murder
Made clean only by time and distance.
Casualties innocent are forgiven by error
Listen now listen
The rain begins (Death-stink-dawn)
Arms still move, legs still walk
Survival is all, just survival.
I met Nghiem later
We were both old men.

We talked, had a drink together.
His wife very pretty with a whiney voice.
He believes he could have
Killed us at any time except for his leaders.
Just what he thinks
War is over."
I break away from his hold
No time no time
I'm going to visit the Memorial.

memories of war

We were so beautiful, we the young,
We were the chosen, the fire makers.
Oh God! Did we have the power.
The battles with the noise, the overpowering din,
Lashing out in physical waves of pain.
The smell of the burnt powder;
The agony of the wounded;
My rifle, hot, beating at me;
Now the fear, wild, fierce, growing fear,
Then suddenly the silence.
Blood roaring through my body,
The powerful total-male feeling,
The joy, the pure joy of survival.
Against all odds, any odds, survival.

Now I'm forced to bow down to boredom.
To the great god tedium, Fascinator.
Ten thousand thousand platitudes
For cash to eat, to sleep, for work.
For the rest of my life this?
No. Instead always this;
I will force life to rise from under me
Like the wonderful whore she is;
And I will reclaim the beauty of battle.

about the author

David is a former US Navy Corpsman who spent time attached to the Marine Corps. He earned a bachelor's degree from North-western College and a master's degree from Western Illinois University. He currently re-sides in Port Saint Lucie, Florida with his wife and three dogs.

the author in Vietnam in 1968

www.ingramcontent.com/pod-product-compliance
Lightning Source LLC
Chambersburg PA
CBHW032046180726
48284CB00008B/2771